W9-CBL-264

For my Mother - Jean Fisher
- M.F.

For my Father - Arnold Peace
- P.L.

For Susanna O'Donnell from Upper Feeny
- B.O'D.

First published in Ireland by O'Donnell Press 2010
12 Coolemoyne Park, Jordanstown, Co. Antrim BT37 0RP
Telephone: 028 9096 6493
Email: b.odonnell93@ntlworld.com
www.odonnellpress.com

Special thanks to Paul Porter & Heather Gracey

A CIP catalogue record of this book is available from the British Library.

Printed in Ireland by GPS Colour Graphics Ltd.

ISBN 978-0-9553325-9-3

1 2 3 4 5 6 7 8 9 10

O'DONNELL PRESS

The Mystery of the Avoca pony

By Mel Fisher

Illustrated by Patricia Ludlow

Nuala stroked Midnight's neck and whispered, "See you soon." Jumping down into the sand she ran across the arena to meet Conor and Rusty.
"Come on slow coach, you'd live here if they'd let you," teased Conor. Her riding lesson was over and she and her brother had a busy day ahead scavenging in the old copper mines.

Nuala and Conor lived in the beautiful village of Avoca, right in the heart of the Wicklow Mountains. Rain or shine, they loved to scramble up into the surrounding hills with Rusty their adorable cocker spaniel.

They followed the river up past the Avoca mill and then climbed the steep slopes to the copper mines. Rusty sniffed around, his red coat almost camouflaged against the red earth.
"Conor listen! Can you hear her?" Nuala whispered, certain she could hear a pony close by.
"No, you're hearing things," he replied bluntly.

Nuala turned away in a huff while Conor kicked the red dirt.

“Whoosh!” the noise made Nuala spin round to look for Conor. Both he and Rusty had disappeared.
“Stop playing tricks, Conor,” said Nuala. But there was silence.
“Rusty!” she shouted, knowing their pet could never stay quiet for long. But again there was nothing.

The silence was uneasy. Nuala stared at her feet, tears welling up in her eyes and she shook her head angrily.
“Brothers!” she snorted. Conor was always playing tricks but this was too much. “Conor, I’m going home. This isn’t a game!”

A muffled cry stopped her in her tracks. It was Conor's voice!
"Conor, where are you?" Trying to keep calm, Nuala could feel a wave of panic rising up inside her.
"I think we've fallen down a mine shaft," he replied.
"Conor, keep talking! I can't see any sign...," her voice faded out as just in front of her she saw a gaping hole.

Kneeling down beside it she called, “Conor!”
An excited bark and a muffled, “Nuala,” rushed up to meet her.
“Are you ok?” asked Nuala, spotting an old rope coiled round a tree trunk and wondering if it might help pull them out of the mine.
“I can’t stand up, my ankle is twisted,” replied Conor shakily.

Nuala closed her eyes and sighed. How was she going to get her injured brother up a rickety old mine shaft? Just then she felt a gentle nudge on her shoulder, and the sweet smell of chewed grass drifting past her nose. Feeling the soft, velvety muzzle of a pony against her face, she turned around, and found herself standing face to face with a striking grey, Connemara pony.

As Nuala stared into the gentle, brown eyes, she realised this pony could help get Conor and Rusty out of the deep mine. Quickly Nuala fed the rope down to Conor, explaining what was happening.

"Conor, tie the rope to your belt! We'll pull you and Rusty up."
"Ok," came a weak voice.
"Give two gentle tugs when you're ready."
Nuala wrapped the rope around the pony and waited for the signal.
One, two tugs. Conor was ready. Slowly the pony started walking. Nuala's face peered down the hole, she could hear them getting closer but it was hard to make anything out in the darkness.

Suddenly Rusty's fur tickled her face and a big wet tongue licked her cheek. He jumped out of Conor's arms and crashed into Nuala delighted to be free. Red mud streaked across his pale face, Conor wasn't in such good shape but he managed a smile as Nuala reached for his hand and pulled him onto the grass.

Nuala went to check the pony. “Good girl,” she whispered, stroking her nose and releasing the rope. She led her over to meet Conor. With a twisted and swollen ankle walking was going to be impossible. The pony was their only hope of getting Conor down from the mines.

The pony stood still while Nuala helped Conor mount the pony bareback. Holding onto the pony's mane, Conor was carried down the slopes with Nuala gently leading her. Rusty seemed to be none the worse for wear, bounding alongside them. They made their way home, trotting down the main street right to their front door. Nuala helped Conor dismount.

"You two are a sight for sore eyes. What have you been up to?" said their mum as she opened the door.
Words tumbled out so quickly their mum could only pick out a few, "mine shaft…. ankle…. pony."
"What pony?" asked their mum.
"This pony," said Nuala as she turned to introduce her mum to the Connemara pony. Nuala looked up and down the street, but the pony had disappeared. Mum helped Conor into the house, and Nuala flopped down on the doorstep, puzzled. But as she listened in the stillness she was sure she could hear the sound of hooves echoing through the valley. Nuala smiled. She knew her mysterious pony was real!